The Lone Raja

A book by m.d head

Vikram Kumar lived in New Delhi, along with his successful family.His mother and father both worked at one of the many fine hospitals in the area.

They had sent him to the best schools and made sure he went to the right university to study medical sciences.All he had to do was get the required results and he would join them.

Vikram always tried his very best to please his doting parents who had given their only son the best of everything,as they had tried so hard for a baby when first married.

One day though after numerous tries they succeeded and vowed that their son would be their crowning glory.From the day he was born anything he desired was his for the taking.All he had to do was get those results.......

In the university quarters, however, Vikram had his own ideas about his future.From the time he was old enough to read and watch television he loved the cowboys.

Not that there was anything remotely similar as such where he lived.His country was such a rich and vibrant place to live and work but Vikram didn't want a regular or prominent job.He wanted to be a Cowboy.

He wanted to be one so much he even ordered an outfit and toy guns from a place he found online, and had it sent to his quarters at the university.

His friends he shared with were always ordering various things anyway so nobody took any notice.One evening his friends went out to the local bars so Vikram was on his own.

He locked his door and quickly tried on his outfit.It was perfect.He then spent the next half hour practising with his toy guns and lasso.

Once he was satisfied he put the outfit away and opened up his laptop.He had found a touring circus online that specialised in Wild West shows.

He spent part of the year performing and part of the year training the performers.It would also teach you how to ride a horse.Vikram thought this was perfect.He just needed to convince his parents then he was off to join the Circus........

At the weekend Vikram phoned his parents to say he would be over as he had some important news to share.His father wondered if his son had finally found himself a wife or at least someone to settle down with.

His mother thought the same and was even thinking of baby names in case that was also something to announce.The whole morning they spent surmising what exactly this important news could be and even made a special meal just incase.His father thought maybe Vikram had passed his exams and that was the reason.

Soon there was a knock on the door of their apartment.Vikram rarely rang the doorbell as it always played the same ghastly classical music his parents loved.Vikram would have preferred something a little modern personally but there it was.

As they fought over who would open it first, the door opened.Both parents stood at the doorway with great beaming smiles upon their faces.

Both hoping to hear their desired expectation.Vikram walked through to the dining room and sat down at the table.He handed his back pack to his mother, who hung it on the coat stand, as his father placed a coffee in front of him.

They then joined their son at the table and looked at him expectantly."Well, we're waiting young man." His father said."Yes dear, we've been waiting patiently all morning since you called." His mother told him.

"This food looks great guys, I hope I deserve it." He said laughing."Oh of course you do, you're our only son who makes us so proud every day." His mother said as his father just raised his eyebrows, bereft.

"Calm down, he's only announcing some news, it's not as if he's had one of these 'life changing moments' and has decided to do something ridiculous, like, I don't know, join the circus for instance. throwing his medical training away,hey."   He said laughing.

"No, we've made sure young Vikram has had the very best education money can buy so I'm sure he could never disappoint us."He said, smiling warmly at his treasured son.

This was the moment when Vikram, who was six foot with an athletic physique to match, suddenly felt very small.This was something he rarely felt as he was naturally gifted with good looks and confidence.Unfortunately when it came to 'knowingly' disappointing his parents all that disappeared......

How, in the name of Shiva, was he going to explain to his parents his announcement.Then he took a breath and thought about it."Mother, father, I respect everything you have worked so hard to achieve and appreciate all you have bestowed upon me.

Without your loving support I wouldn't be half the man I am today, so I thank you. You have been so amazing with your love and generosity it humbles me to my very core."

He then nodded to himself as if to subconsciously approve of what he was going to say."Yes," He thought,that's perfect.

"WELL." His parents both asked, 'slightly' annoyed now.Taken aback a little, Vikram 'actually' said "I'm going to be a......."Before he had a chance to say his parents jumped in."A Doctor".His father said."A nurse."Said his mother."Noooooo, I'm going to be a.............Cowboy!!!!"

With that he pulled a cowboy hat from his backpack and placed it on his head.His parents just looked stunned, then looked at each other, still stunned.

For the rest of the day silence was the only thing 'heard' in the apartment.Vikram's parents explained how they felt about his decision.None of it was particularly positive or intact.

Suffice to say they were not.... 'in ore' of his announcement.He was going to try to reason with them, that his decision wouldn't affect his medical training, but knew it was pointless.

He just told them he respected their opinion and let himself out.He stepped out into the cool night air and breathed in, slowly, then exhaled.Of Course, He could have told them his other news that he had passed all of his medical exams 'with flying colours'.

He couldn't be bothered though so just readjusted his hat and strolled off into the night.The next day, early, he emailed the circus and waited for a reply.

While he waited he packed a few things and wrote his parents a letter.He tried to convey to them how much they meant to him.That he hoped they could still be proud of him, even though he wanted to take another path in life.

Once he was happy with what he wrote he decided to try on his outfit one more time.He wanted to make sure he looked as good as he could.

Hopefully if the boss of the circus saw how much effort he had put into it, it might go in his favour.Of Course, that was if the circus even got back to him.

Then there was a metallic tune being played that let him know the circus had replied. Vikram opened the laptop and found the email. Not only did they say he'd been accepted but he was the first person from India to play a cowboy in their circus.

The Circus would be passing through New Delhi in the next few days, where Vikram could meet up with the crew. There he would be introduced to the rest of the employees and told what to expect.

He would be given a months trial and if he passed he would be given a contract for a year.This was it, he was going to be a cowboy, riding horses, firing guns and performing rope tricks.Or so he thought.........

On the day the circus turned up Vikram arrived at the front of the big top with his backpack and outfit.The owner was a white guy in his 70's who looked a bit like some of the characters on the tv shows Vikram used to watch.

"Hello young man, now why the hell would a wealthy modern young man like yourself want to join a circus?" He asked.

Vikram explained to him why it was so important to him and the owner just nodded."Okay then,enjoy the show and you can leave when the show ends.

With that, Vikram joined the rest of the people heading inside the big top tent.Within minutes all his senses were awoken as he could see flaming clubs being juggled and hear animals roaring.

He could feel the heat from the fiery clubs aswell as the cool breeze that slipped inside the big top.He could almost taste the sweet smelling popcorn being sold as people munched on it.

Almost distracting you from the back stage crew.The owner then appeared in the centre of the three rings.Dressed in the red, white and blue of America and wearing a large cowboy hat, with stars all over it.

The three rings were big enough to house a small circus in 'each' and Vikram wondered where the Wild West part of the show would be held, or in fact 'when'.

That was when he heard it......."NOW,LADIES AND GENTLEMEN,BOYS AND GIRLS." The ringmaster boomed out as hooves could be heard stomping on the ground."Introducing the newest acquisition to my Circus, The Wild West Experience."

As he finished his speech four horses came galloping into the ring, rode by two women and two men, dressed as cowboys.The cowgirls began doing tricks on their horses while the cowboys began shooting wildly with their six shooters(guns) in various directions.

Suddenly the cowgirls began swinging their ropes and made lassoes to snag the cowboys, still shooting their guns   as a lone cowboy dressed in white, wearing a mask walked into the ring.

He pulled out his irons(guns) and fired at the cowboys who watched their gun belts drop to the dusty floor,followed by their guns.Then, they were dragged away from the rings by the cowgirls.

The masked man jumped upon the two riderless horses and rode around the rings before riding out of the big top itself.The audiences cheered and clapped as the lights went out for a few minutes then came back on.

The performers were now standing alongside the ringmaster and taking their bows."This will be the last time Deek Rivers will be playing our 'masked man' ladies and gentlemen as he retires today.Lets give him a big hand now."

With that the whole of the big top erupted into a cacophony of noise.Vikram knew he had definitely made the right decision there and then.

After the show was over Vikram met up with the performers and helped pack up.It was important he made the right impression as he hoped to be with them for quite a while.

Once all the packing was done everything was loaded into huge tractor rigs(lorries).There were two 'rigs' and a large camper van that was for the performers and behind the scenes staff.

Vikram and the rest of the crew jumped in the vehicles and set off.Where to exactly Vikram didn't know but what he did know was that he could not wait to start his training.

For the next few months Vikram was trained in a whole manner of disciplines from horse riding to learning to use a gun.

The rope tricks were particularly hard to manage,but over time became quite easy to achieve.He was even taught how to ride two horses at the same time.

Deek Rivers, the original masked cowboy who had retired,taught him how to do the gun tricks.By the end of the training,Vikram was not only competent in all the disciplines,he excelled at them.

Soon it was his first performance in the ring.He asked if could wear his outfit he bought online.The ring leader said he could and Vikram wore part of Deeks outfit too out of respect.

Once he was fully dressed it looked awesome.Vikram wore the black trousers and shirt from his own outfit, aswell as the white gloves, boots and hat from Deeks.

He finished it all off with a white coloured leather gun belt,covered with shiny rhinestones.Deek even gave Vikram his own guns to use.

They had pearl handles and were so well polished, they sparkled as Vikram eased them out their holsters.

Vikram then slid the black eye mask into place so the only parts of his face you could see was his nose, mouth and strong jawline.

As he was about to walk into the ring he heard

a familiar sound.It was the pure black stallion

he had trained on.

Leading it towards him was Deke Rivers."You look the part kid, now let's see you ride out on your 'steed'.He said smiling warmly.Vikram got himself into the saddle and walked Javelin into the ring as the lights slowly went up.

As the lights came on fully all the metallic parts of Vikram's costume and the rhinestones sparkled,as the audience took an intake of breath, at the vision that appeared.Vikram felt untouchable as he rode Javelin around each of the rings, performing various tricks he had learnt.

Then the ringleader's voice boomed through the bull horn."LADIES AND GENTLEMEN, BOYS AND GIRLS, please allow me to introduce to you The Lone Raja." Vikram loved his new name as he was a fan of The Lone Ranger Anyway.

He slipped underneath Javelin, while still sitting in the saddle, and fired off a few shots.There was a sudden burst of light as three flares released red,white and blue plumes of smoke into the air.

Vikram then righted himself so he was now sitting astride the mighty Javelin and began galloping around the rings as two more cowboys entered the big top.

They began shooting wildly into the air as Vikram untied his rope and lassoed both of them and jumped off his steed.He tied the two cowboys together and jumped upon their horse.

The audience then watched in awe as the masked cowboy rode the riderless horses out of the ring as he whistled a unique tune.

Suddenly Javelin charged towards the tied up cowboys and scooped them up, carrying them by their blinding.The audience gasped as he carried them out of the ring.

As Vikram listened to the crowd he decided there and then he had made the right choice.After the show ended Vikram made his way to the camper van to get changed."Excuse me sir, can I have a selfie." The voice asked as Vikram turned around.

The voice belonged to a small Indian girl whose smile stretched from ear to ear as Vikram stood beside her for the selfie.``Oh wow, I got a selfie with The Lone Raja ''. She exclaimed as she ran off to her parents, who were waiting for her by their car.The small girl waved him goodbye as Vikram strolled back to the camper van,smiling...........THE END...........